Ever wish you had all the money for everything you needed ... and everything you wanted? I'm talking *everything:* a top-of-the-line Fender Stratocaster guitar, all the smoothies you can drink, the entire stock of Lip Gloss Emporium. ... Okay, maybe that's everything *I* ever wanted. But you get the idea. I mean, I know they say that money can't buy you everything — but just try paying for that new pair of jeans with anything else. Love? Kindness? Monopoly dollars? No luck. Down at the mall they only take cold hard cash.

And I should know, because I've been stopping by the mall a lot lately. That's "a lot" as in, the amount of money I no longer have, thanks to all those jeans and smoothies.

Here's what it comes down to: I was broke. Flat

broke, unable to buy that new Sizzling Sunrise lip gloss I wanted or even a pitiful cup of juice! So I figured there was only one solution to my problems: money. If I could just find a way to make some — or, even better, make a lot — then all my problems would be solved.

Turns out it's not so easy.

They may be right that money can't buy you everything — but as I found out, it can sure buy you a whole lot of trouble!

But let's back up to that day a few weeks ago when I learned the sad truth about my empty wallet. I was sitting in *Juice!* with my best friends in the world, Geena Fabiano and Zach Carter-Schwartz. We go to *Juice!* almost every day after school, partly because it's so bright and funky inside, partly because all the other kids from our school hang out there, too — but mainly because the smoothies are just so awesome. I mean, you've never tasted fruit like this. Sometimes I'd get distracted all day just thinking about the cool, delicious smoothie I'd get as soon as the bell rang.

And that day was one of those days.

I was a little late, so Zach and Geena were already there, gulping down their drinks, when I raced in and grabbed a seat at our usual table. "I'm in a Berry Bomber mood today," I mused as I dug through my purse. Just one problem: My purse was empty. Unless you count my cell phone, my house keys, a rubber band, and three pieces of fuzz. None of which were going to be of much help in buying me that Berry Bomber. "I coulda sworn I had enough," I muttered. No matter — who needs cash when you've got friends? "Zach, could you spot me a couple of —"

"Bucks?" Zach finished for me, and I realized he already had his wallet out. Weird.

"How'd you know I was gonna ask that?"

Zach rolled his eyes. "Come on. You're always sponging off me."

"No, I'm not," I protested. But I was starting to get a bad feeling — you know, like when you're pretty sure the teacher's about to announce a pop quiz, and even though she hasn't officially done it yet, you can already feel your stomach start to sink. "Uh . . . am I?"

That's when Zach led me on a little trip down memory lane. Kind of a "This Is Your Life, Addie Singer" — or maybe more like "This is Your Cash Flow Problem, Addie Singer."

There's Addie at the mall holding up a pair of long, dangly earrings — incidentally, earrings that, once she owned them, went straight to the bottom of her drawer, never to be worn: "I can't live without these! Loan me the money and I promise I'll pay you back."

Here's Addie studying a big poster board of tournament seedings: "Duane's got a pool going to see when your basketball team will get knocked out of the state tournament. Can I borrow some cash? I promise I'll pay you back."

And last, but not least . . . okay, definitely least, there's Addie in one of those stores full of sparkly junk, holding up a hermit crab painted bright pink. "This hermit crab matches my phone! Lend me the money to buy it. . . . I'll name him after you."

"Okay. So maybe Lil Zachy hermit crab was pushing it," I admitted, grinning sheepishly. When you put it like that, all together in one big list, of course it was going to sound like I was always sponging off of Zach. And I guess I *did* borrow more money from him than I realized. "But I promise to pay you back!"

"You couldn't even if you wanted to," Zach warned me. "It would take you your whole life."

"It can't be that much."

"I'm going to write the number down on this piece of paper." Zach grabbed a napkin and scribbled something down, then folded it up and slid it across the table to me.

I unfolded it and saw what he'd written. Hey, no big deal — I could definitely save up my allowance for a while and pay him back. "That's not so bad."

That's when Zach reached over and unfolded the rest of the napkin, revealing another zero, and another, until I saw the *whole* number I owed him. Let's just say it filled up the whole napkin — let's just say if I had that much cash, it probably would have filled up the whole inside of *Juice!* Not that it mattered, because I would *never, ever* be able to come up with that much cash. Zach was right, it would take my whole life. I was doomed!

"How come you let me borrow so much?" I just couldn't believe it was possible — had I really spent *that* much money?

Zach shrugged. "You kept promising to pay me back."

"Where'd you get all that money to loan her, anyway?" Geena asked. "Are you secretly rich?"

"No, I just know how to handle my finances responsibly," Zach bragged. "I don't blow it all on earrings and hermit crabs." Then he looked across the table at me and the truth sank in. "Actually . . . I guess I do."

I took a deep breath. "Well, it's only money, right?" Would they fall for that one?

"Actually, no, it's not only money," Geena countered. And she started listing all the things I'd borrowed from her: her earrings, her cute new tank top, her designer sunglasses. . . . It just went on and on and on. "And you never give them back!"

I wanted to slide under the table and disappear — my friends were right, I was totally sponging off of them. And I hadn't even noticed!

"Okay!" I said loudly, in the middle of Geena's tirade. "I get it. I borrow from you guys too much. But I promise to pay you back." I just wasn't sure how.

"With what?" Zach asked, looking doubtful. "Homemade coupons for a foot massage?"

"Ew, no." Geena cringed. "She can ask her dad for a raise in her allowance."

My dad? You need the Jaws of Life to pry money out of his wallet. "I don't know if he'll go for that," I warned them. Understatement of the month.

"Sure he will," Geena said confidently. "Tell him you need money for 'girl things.'" She whispered that last part, as if it was some kind of code and I was supposed to know exactly what she meant. Not so much.

"What 'girl things'?"

"Trust me." Geena gave me a serene smile as if it

was already a done deal. "He won't want to know the specifics."

Juice! is a great place when I just want to get away from it all — unless I want to get away from my big brother, Ben. Then it's exactly the wrong place to be, because now Ben works there. That's right, my annoying big brother, trespassing on *my* turf! It's not all bad, though — every once in a while I get a discount on my smoothie. That is, I *used* to get discounts, back in the day when I could still afford to buy smoothies. And sometimes, if I'm really, really lucky, I get to watch Ben make a total idiot of himself.

It doesn't happen that often — after all, Ben's pretty much Mr. Perfect. And he knows it, which is the most annoying thing of all. But that week — the week I discovered my wallet was empty — Ben had been making a fool of himself a lot more often.

For example, just as I was promising Zach I would pay him back, Ben was behind the counter, chatting up some cute high school girls. Or rather, they were chatting up each other — Ben turned on all the charm he had, but it didn't seem to make much difference.

"So I told her if she didn't like it, she could get

lost," one of the girls was saying, as Ben slid her juice across the counter.

"That'll be four seventy-five and your seven-digit phone number," he said, giving her the smarmy grin that girls usually go crazy for. "Ten digits with the area code."

Usually, this is the point in the story where I get nauseous — nothing grosses me out more than seeing Ben make girls melt. But this time? Things went a little differently. This time the girls didn't even bother to look up.

"So she just said, fine, make me get lost," the girl continued to her friend, sliding a five-dollar bill across the counter. Then they both grabbed their glasses and wandered away, as if Ben didn't exist.

The newest employee, some girl who was in Ben's class at school and seemed to have the same opinion of him I did, snuck up behind him and shook her head. "Crash and burn," she said, letting out a long whistle that ended in a big explosion.

I couldn't have said it better myself.

"Fifth one today," the girl said incredulously. "And everyone said Ben Singer was such a Romeo."

Ben glowered, the color creeping into his cheeks the way it always does right before he wrestles me to the ground and steals the remote. But I guess you can't really wrestle in the workplace. So he just waved her away, growling, "Back to your blender, trainee!"

That afternoon, I might have lost all my cash, but Ben had lost something way more crucial: his mojo.

As soon as my dad got home, I tried out Geena's plan. And you know what? It worked! Well . . . almost.

Just like Geena suggested, I asked Dad for some extra allowance money to buy "girl things."

"Which things?" he asked, backing away like he didn't really want to know. He was blinking really fast and I was pretty sure I saw some beads of sweat on his forehead. I've got to hand it to Geena — when she's right, she's right.

"Girl things," I said, trying to convince myself it wasn't a total lie. After all, paying Zach back for dangling earrings is sort of a "girl thing." At least, I was a girl — and this was my thing. "You know, things like —"

"I only have fifties," Dad said, whipping out his wallet and cutting me off before I could go into detail. I was *so* close, and then —

"*Wait!*" Mom was sitting at the kitchen table looking over some blueprints, but I could tell by the way she narrowed her eyes and glared at me that she'd heard

9

every word. Looks like Ben's love life wasn't the only thing that was going to crash and burn. "Asking for 'girl things' is the oldest trick in the book. What do you *really* need the money for?"

I sighed. I guess honesty is the best policy. Well, no, obviously telling your dad that you need to buy "girl things" and doing it when your mom is *not home* is the best policy. But honesty was a good runner-up.

"Well, Mommy," I began sweetly, hoping that if I smiled and made my eyes really wide I could wake up that part of Mom that just wants to protect her little babies from the cold hard world, "I borrowed a lot of stuff from Geena and Zach and I need to pay them back."

"Sorry, honey, but all our extra money is tied up in these renovations." She pointed to the blueprints, which showed how the new room was going to be attached to the rest of the house. "If you need more money, you'll just have to do what Ben did." He came into the room just as she said it. Great. Nothing Ben likes to hear more than one of our parents telling me to be more like him. I'd be hearing about this one for a long time.

"Defraud Grandma?" I asked dubiously.

"She *gave* me those coins!" Ben protested.

Yeah, right.

"What your mom is saying is that you could get a job," Dad explained.

"Addie, work?" Ben snorted in disbelief. "Father, please. Work requires focus, dedication, and responsibility. Remember the one-and-only time she tried to make dinner?"

Okay, was it really my fault that I almost set the kitchen on fire? I mean, I was doing a nice thing, right, offering to make dinner for my family? And they're going to throw it back in my face *just because* I got distracted talking on the phone to Geena and let the pot boil over? I mean, she was having a shoe crisis, what was I supposed to do? And just because I left the burner on when I took the pot away, does that make me irresponsible? Just because I threw a dish towel on the burner and accidentally started a fire that probably would have burned our house down if our brilliant dog, Nancy, hadn't dragged out the hose and put it out just in time, does that make me a complete and total spaz? Does that make me incapable of completing even a simple task without it turning into a total disaster?

Uh . . . can I plead the Fifth?

"If it hadn't been for Nancy, we'd be living on the streets," Ben pointed out.

"That was a long time ago. I'm older now. I can handle a job."

"You could always work with your father at the store," Mom suggested. Dad owns a sporting-goods store — that could be fun, I figured. Or at least, not totally heinous. I started to nod, when Dad almost spit out the water he'd just gulped down.

"No!" he yelled. Then quickly continued, ". . . positions available. We're totally staffed up."

A likely story. The truth was obvious: Even my own father didn't think I could hold down a job.

"Fine," I said, determined to prove them all wrong. "I can earn my own money another way. You'll see."

Usually when I have a big problem to figure out, I go up to my room, pull out my guitar, and make up a song about my troubles. It almost always helps me sort things out and figure out what I should do. Not this time. This time I grabbed my guitar and took it down to the center of town, where I planted myself on a corner and started playing.

I'm really down-and-out singing on the street.
I got holes in my pockets in my designer jeans.

Brother, spare me a dime . . .
'Cause I need money. . . .

Okay, it wasn't the best song I'd ever written. But you know what? It worked! Right away, someone walking by dropped some coins in my guitar case. A few more like that — well, a few thousand more like that — and I'd have it made.

Unfortunately, I never got that far. The next person to walk by was a cop . . . and he didn't just keep on walking.

"You have a permit for street performance?" the officer asked, like he already knew the answer.

"Permit? I didn't know you needed a permit!" I gave him my best wide-eyed innocent look — but I guess when you're a cop, you've seen that plenty of times before. Because he didn't seem to care.

"Ignorance of the law is no excuse for breaking it," he said sternly, and handed me a ticket.

"It's *how* much?" I asked incredulously, my eyes practically bugging out of my head. Now I owed the government almost as much as I owed Zach!

"See there?" The officer shook his head. "A permit woulda been cheaper."

*   *   *

Take Two. So what if the whole music career didn't work out — I had other talents.

The next day I came to school equipped with a basket full of delicious goodies. "Come get your home-made sandwiches!" I called out to anyone passing by me in the halls. "Made by . . . Addie Singer!"

Everything was going pretty well at first — well, I didn't actually have any customers, but I was pretty sure I'd spotted a couple of people who *looked* hungry. Kind of. Then Principal Brandywine zoomed up on her motorized scooter and spoiled the whole thing.

"Addie Singer!" she snapped, waggling her finger at me — she looked like she was itching to hand me a detention slip right then and there. "What do you think you're doing?"

"Selling sandwiches?" It seemed pretty obvious to me.

"We have a health-board–certified cafeteria! This is a public school, not a taco shack in Tijuana! Pack up your basket, I'm shutting you down."

Strike two.

Next, I tried a dog wash, figuring that would *have* to work. Who doesn't want a clean dog, right? And I love dogs, especially clean ones. It was a match made in heaven. Soon, I figured, I'd have all the cash I could ever need.

"Dog wash!" I cried out to passersby, pointing to the sign I'd made. "Big and small, I wash 'em all!"

The first person who came along had a very familiar face. A face I'd hoped never to see again.

"Don't tell me I need a permit for this?" I asked the officer, my heart sinking.

"Nah, I'm just in need of some dog-washing services. I'll make your ticket go away. . . ."

And just like that, I could breathe again. For washing one dog, I could at least get rid of some of my debt — and I had plenty of time to make even more money. "Okay!"

"My K-9 squad's getting kinda stinky," he said, sticking two fingers in his mouth and whistling. "Here, boys!"

Did he say "squad"?

Did he say "boys"?

A second later, a German shepherd came racing toward us, with another one following right behind. And then another. And another. And another

Let's just say that by the time I got through washing the whole *squad*, the day was over — and I never wanted to see another dog again.

Plus, I hadn't even made a cent.

So much for being an entrepreneur. Three strikes and I was out.

Ain't got no money, owe my friends a load, I sang, once I got back to my bedroom, dirty and dejected.

Went looking for a job, it was a long, hard road.
Tried singin' and a-sellin'
Got stinky and soaked.
Now I'm sudsy, sad, and still broke.

"I guess the dog washing didn't go so well," Mom guessed, stopping in my doorway as she passed down the hall.

"I didn't make a penny," I complained. "And I'll smell like hound for days."

"I just sold a condo to a man who's new in town and needs a babysitter for his little girl. Do you think you'd —"

"I'll do it!" I shouted, jumping up from the bed. Was she kidding? This was a miracle! The perfect job, coming along just when I needed it the most. "Thank you!" I threw my arms around her and hugged her tight, but after a minute, she wriggled out of my grasp.

"Uh . . . honey? You mind?" she asked, scrunching up her nose. "Your stench is making me dizzy."

Nancy barked and covered up her nose with her paws. Great. I'd already taken two showers, and even the *dog* thought I smelled too much like dog.

"Sorry, Mom." I backed away. "Sorry, Nancy."

But it didn't matter. I'd shower a hundred times, if that's what it took to wash the stink away. Suddenly, I felt like I could do anything. And why? Because I had found the perfect job! I should have thought of it before: babysitting. What better way was there for someone like me to make a fast buck? I'd just go over to the kid's house, watch a little TV, maybe braid her hair, and . . . *poof*! Good-bye, money problems — hello, big spender. All without lifting a finger.

After all, I figured, how hard could babysitting one little girl be?

If I had only known . . .

She was four feet tall.

She was totally adorable.

And I was pretty sure she was possessed.

Not that her head was spinning around or any-thing, but still, there was something unnatural about her. I mean, what five-year-old girl runs back and forth across the living room, screaming at the top of her lungs for fifteen minutes straight? I've seen sugar highs before, but to be on that much of a sugar high she would have had to eat a candy bar taller than she was.

Which, come to think of it, I wouldn't have put past her.

"It's been eight months since Scarlett's mother was shipped overseas," her father, Mr. Corn, explained to me. He looked more like it had been eight years — and he also looked about ready to pass out. I was getting a funny feeling about this whole babysitting thing — like maybe it wasn't quite so perfect as I'd thought. "Only one more month till she gets back!"

That's when Scarlett clambered up onto the arm of the sofa and put herself into a diver's pose. "I'm gonna fly off the sofa, Daddy!" she announced at top volume. A few more minutes of this and I was going to go deaf.

"No, sweetie." Mr. Corn sighed and scooped her off the couch. "We don't mess up the nice white sofa. Your mother loves this sofa. Why don't you put on your princess outfit?"

Scarlett took a deep breath and held it. Her face got redder and redder, and her lips puckered, until finally, she exploded, "I! HATE! PRINCESSES!" And then, as all the air whooshed out of her body, she deflated, like a burst water balloon, and stomped off to her room.

Mr. Corn rubbed the back of his head and looked down at the rug. He seemed a bit nervous, and I could guess why. "So, uh, as you can see, my little Scarlett's a bit of a handful."

Oomph. Before I could answer, something flew across the room and hit me in the stomach. It bounced off me and I caught it: a sparkly princess tiara.

Scarlett might not have been much of a princess, but she was quite a pitcher. Ouch.

"She's very sweet once you get to know her," Mr. Corn claimed. Yeah, right.

Scarlett hadn't come out of the bedroom yet, but it seemed pretty obvious that she wasn't putting on her princess outfit, so what was she —

"I'm gonna fly into the TV to be with Dora the Explorer!"

Before either of us could do anything, there was a pause, and then a huge crash. With all the thuds and the breaking glass, it sounded like . . . well, it sounded like a crazy five-year-old had just launched herself into the TV screen.

Mr. Corn looked pretty crazed himself — he was forcing himself to smile, but there was desperation in his eyes. I felt kind of bad for him. But not bad enough to stick around. It was obvious I was the only sane one left in this apartment — and I planned to stay that way!

"Uh, I'm not sure . . ." I began, wondering how to politely phrase what I needed to say next, which was, *your child is a freakish terror and I wouldn't babysit her for all the money in the world.*

"Look, I really need a babysitter," Mr. Corn said, talking fast as if he knew I had one foot out the door. "I'm gonna write a number down, and if it's high enough for you, the job is yours." He scribbled something on a piece of paper, folded it, and slid it across the coffee table. I figured it would be polite to look — I could at least *pretend* I was going to consider his offer before walking out the door forever.

So I unfolded the paper.

And gasped.

I had to look again, just to make sure I hadn't read it wrong, or miscounted all those zeroes. And then I looked a third time, because it didn't seem possible.

I took a deep breath. "I'm your girl!" I cried — and even though a tiny part of me was wondering what I was getting myself into, I ignored it. Because for the amount written on that paper, I could handle one little kid, no matter how wild. I could handle anything.

It wasn't all the money in the world.

But it was close.

Back home, Ben was still looking for his lost mojo. And by looking, I mean he was staring at himself in the mirror, thinking how beautiful he was and wondering how any girl could have turned him down. Ben does this about two hours every day — he says he's just admiring one of the wonders of the world.

And because he spent so much time looking at himself in the mirror, because he had memorized every freckle, every dimple, every pore on his flawless face, Ben saw it almost immediately. A tiny red imperfection, a blemish, a — no, it couldn't be. It couldn't possibly be that.

So he decided to ignore the problem and hope it would go away.

It didn't.

In fact, it got bigger. Redder. Oozier.

And by dinner that night, he was pretty sure he could feel it pulsing, throbbing, destroying his smooth, perfect face.

"Mom, call Dr. Kaychuck," he said, examining his reflection in the butter knife. "I have chicken pox."

"Relax," Mom said, after taking a quick look at the red spot on Ben's chin. "It's not chicken pox. It's probably just a pimple."

Wrong answer. Or rather, right answer — wrong way to deliver the bad news. Ben freaked out.

"There's no way I have a pimple! I don't get pimples. A pimple is so beyond not cool. I'm sure it's a beauty mark." Ben nodded, mentally talking himself into the idea. "Yeah, that's it, a beauty mark."

He looked so relieved, so happy to have solved his problem, that I just had to say something. After all, what are little sisters for?

"That is not a beauty mark, you freak," I pointed out. "Beauty marks are dark."

"How do you know, are you a beauty-ologist?"

"No, I'm a babysitter." I glowed with the memory of that little piece of paper and all those zeroes. I'd spent all afternoon planning how I was going to spend my newfound fortune. "You should see how much Mr. Corn is paying me!" I scrawled the amount down on a piece of paper and slid it across to Mom. Her eyes almost bugged out of her head when she saw the number.

"I should've asked for a bigger commission," she mumbled to herself. Then she frowned. "Addie, nobody pays this much unless there's a catch. You sure you can handle this?"

Was I *sure*? Well, maybe that was overstating it a little bit. But I was at least *hopeful* that I could deal. Okay, so Scarlett had been a little . . . excited. But maybe that was just a one-time thing. Or maybe she just needed a good babysitter to show her how to behave. Not that I'd ever babysat anyone before. But I was certain I'd be great at it. For what Mr. Corn was paying me, I would have to be! Either way, my family didn't have to know all the details. I didn't need them to worry about whether I could handle things. So I just beamed brightly at Mom. And then I lied through my teeth. "Totally. Scarlett's a little angel."

"Scarlett! You can't put your toys in the blender!" It had been like this all afternoon.

Scarlett, don't put your dirty shoes on the table!
Scarlett, don't climb over the railing on the balcony!
Scarlett, don't turn me into a human pincushion!

And every time I told her not to do something, she managed to find something else even worse. Now she was running toward the kitchen with an armload of dolls and stuffed animals. And she was heading straight for the blender.

Great. Just great. I'd only been there for an hour and already I felt like I'd been through a war. I was dirty, sweaty, every muscle ached, and my voice had gone hoarse from shouting. And there was a desert of time between now and when Mr. Corn was due home.

"Daddy lets me," Scarlett protested, trying to stuff her plush polar bear down into the blender.

"He does *not!*" I pulled out a clipboard, planning to prove it. "Your dad left me specific instructions. 'Don't answer the door to strangers,'" I read. "'Don't take

Scarlett out of the apartment,' and 'Don't let Scarlett put anything in the blender.'"

"Not fair," Scarlett said, throwing the toys down to the ground and stomping her foot.

I know she's a kid and all, and I know she probably misses her mom, but still — what a *brat!*

The doorbell rang. "I'm sorry, but I can't open the door to strangers!" I shouted. The stranger didn't know how lucky he was — the last place anyone in their right mind would want to be was in this apartment with Scarlett.

"Addie Singer?" a familiar voice came through the door.

"Mary Ferry?" I opened the door, and there she was, looking blond and prepared as always. Mary's in my class at school, and she's kind of weird — but she's also totally brilliant. She edits the school newspaper, she aces every science test, and she's dating Duane Ogilvy, who is pretty much the biggest dork this side of the Mississippi. And for some reason, she was standing on Mr. Corn's doorstep, holding an overstuffed portfolio and looking none too happy to see me.

"What are you doing here?" I asked.

"I heard through the grapevine about an available babysitting job. Color me surprised to find *you* here."

I wasn't so sure I liked the sound of that. "What's so 'surprising' about that?"

"Well, you're not exactly the responsible type."

Excuse me? Okay, so maybe I was a little klutzy, and maybe I got a little distracted, *sometimes*, but that certainly did *not* make me irresponsible. And who was Mary to tell me whether or not I could do my job?

"Come on, it's just babysitting."

"Just babysitting?" Mary gave me a smug grin and opened her portfolio. She flipped through page after page of photographs, each one showing a happy, clean, well-behaved child smiling out at the camera. I wondered what Scarlett would do if I tried to take a picture of her. She'd probably try to stick the camera in the blender. And me along with it.

"Joey Simpson, busted his chin on the coffee table. Three stitches," Mary said, pointing to one of the pictures. "Alanis Dougherty, fell off her bike and scraped her knee. Required topical antibiotics."

Then she flipped to the last page of the portfolio, and I almost gagged. It was a newspaper clipping with a photo of Mary Ferry holding a happy little kid. And it was easy to see why he was so happy — the headline read: HERO BABYSITTER!

"Maddie Jericho. Choked on a nickel," Mary

explained. "I administered the Heimlich. See, people call *me* when they need to be sure their children are in good hands."

"Well, you can put that book away. I have everything under control."

What was that sound?

That crunching, whirring, snapping . . . it sounded like . . . a blender.

"Scarlett!"

The blender shut itself off, but I suspected that the damage had been done.

"Under control, huh?" Mary pushed past me into the apartment. Tiny pieces of toys were floating through the air. I guess Scarlett had forgotten to put the top on the blender when she ground up her toys. Even better.

"I'm not surprised that your version of 'under control' looks like this," Mary said patronizingly. She shook her head in disgust. "Total disarray of the work space."

I didn't know what to say to get her out of there, so I just stared at her in silence. She marched across the kitchen and stuck a giant magnet on the refrigerator. It was Mary Ferry's business card, complete with a giant photo of her. I couldn't believe she took babysitting so seriously — I mean, it was just babysitting!

Before I could say anything else, the blender started up again, and a shower of toy parts rained down on us. It was all too much. The final straw was when something landed on my shoulder — I turned to see what it was and found myself staring into the eyes of a tiny pony head.

She'd even stuck her toy ponies in the blender? This was worse than I'd thought.

"My number's on the card," Mary said, totally unfazed by the rain of toys. "Tell the parents they can call me any time they need me." She brushed the pony head off my shoulder like it was nothing. "And they will."

After a few days of sitting for Scarlett, I felt like I'd been put through the spin cycle on a washing machine and then hung out to dry. When Mr. Corn came home from work and sent me away, all I wanted to do was go home and collapse into bed. But one night, Geena and Zach finally dragged me to *Juice!*, claiming they never saw me anymore. One thing about this job stuff, it was really cutting into my social life. Of course, the less time I spent at *Juice!*, the less money I could spend — but less *Juice!* also meant less Zach and Geena, and that meant less fun. So I forced myself to go, even though when we got there, I barely had enough energy to pick up my drink and make it back to the table.

"How's the babysitting?" Geena asked. As if she couldn't tell by the way I was slumped over the table, just waiting for someone to put me out of my misery.

"Scarlett flushed a blanket down the toilet today," I admitted. And it wasn't even the worst thing she'd done that afternoon.

"Man, that kid is out of control," Zach marveled. "You should get another job."

"No way." I sat up straighter, feeling some of my energy return. Just the thought of giving up made me determined to get it together and push forward. "The money's big. I'll be able to pay you guys back in no time." I glanced over at the counter, where Ben was pouring out a drink for yet another pretty blond high school girl. "Besides, Ben thinks I can't handle a job. No way am I giving him the satisfaction of seeing me give up. Not 'Mr. Employee of the Month.'"

Ben had been Employee of the Month every month since he'd started working. He was polite, precise, punctual, pretty much the perfect employee.

I slumped back down on the table again.

It was enough to make anyone sick.

                    *   *   *

Over at the counter, Ben's "beauty mark" hadn't gone away. Instead, it had been fruitful and multiplied — now there were at least three or four little red marks dotting his face. In between serving customers, Ben was examining his reflection in a huge, shiny label, coloring over the zits with a big black marker. I guess he'd believed me after all that beauty marks were dark.

Unfortunately, coloring in zits with a black permanent marker isn't exactly the best way to make yourself beautiful. It is, however, a good way to make yourself look like a Dalmatian.

If Ben's day was already pretty bad, judging from the look on his manager's face, it was about to get worse.

"Ben, I'm afraid that you're not the Employee of the Month," his manager told him, clapping a hand on Ben's shoulder.

"What? Why not? Is it my face?" he asked, stricken. "'Cause they're just beauty marks —"

"Oh." But you could tell that even Manager Mike wasn't fooled by the marker. "I still can't give you EOM. Your sales are down, and your blenders are never shiny. It's like . . . you've lost your touch."

Or his mojo.

"So who's Employee of the Month?"

The manager pointed over to the big gold plaque, which for so long had worn Ben's photo. Now it had a new smiling face peering up from it. She was blond, she was pretty, and Ben would recognize that smug grin anywhere.

"The *trainee*?" He gaped in horror, as the trainee in question snuck up behind him and made her trademark crash-and-burn whistle.

Ben glowered and refused to look at her. So the trainee thought she could get the better of him, steal his mojo *and* his Employee of the Month award? No more fun and games, Ben decided, furiously polishing his blender until it shone like the sun. This was war.

The next day started out like any ordinary day — well, any ordinary day when I was too tired to move because I'd spent the whole night before picking feathers out of my hair, thanks to Scarlett's one-sided pillow fight.

Does it count as a pillow fight when one person is sitting on the sofa while the other, very little, very wild person is bashing her over the head a million times with her father's expensive goose-feather-filled pillows?

No, I didn't think so, either.

31

But anyway, the next morning was fine and normal — until I passed by Duane Ogilvy's locker and spotted something that made me stop in my tracks.

"What's this?" I asked suspiciously, pointing at the giant tote board he'd taped up.

At least Duane had the decency to look a little embarrassed. "It's a pool to see when you'll quit that babysitting job."

What? I glared at Duane. How dare he — and, judging from the board, half the school — bet on my failure?

Duane just shrugged. "It was Mary's idea. But don't feel bad, it's getting a lot of action. . . . You wanna enter?"

The next day after school, Ben trudged into Dad's sporting-goods store. He was drooping like a plant that hadn't been watered in weeks.

Dad put down his stack of shoe boxes as soon as he caught sight of Ben's face. My big brother is always grinning; it's his trademark. So you know that when that frown turns upside down, it's something big. "Ben, what's the matter?"

"I lost a wrestling match," Ben said in a quiet, flat voice.

"Are you all right?"

"I guess." He didn't look it. "But I also lost Employee of the Month. And my beauty marks turned out to be zits. Dad, I'm real worried. I'm losing my touch."

Dad smiled. Not because he didn't feel for Ben —

he just likes to be needed. And now that we're older, we don't come to him for advice all that often. Sometimes parents get kind of insecure, I guess — if you don't ask for their help every once in a while, they start thinking that all you need them for is driving you places and buying you stuff. Not that that's *totally* untrue. "Ben, you're not losing your touch. You're just in a slump!" Uh-oh, I felt a sports analogy coming on. This is the reason why we don't ask Dad for advice too often. For him, every problem has its solution in the world of sports. Sounds okay, I guess, unless you're a seven-year-old girl who wants a new dress for her birthday and your dad starts babbling on about bunting and hitting a home run and taking one for the team and — oh, right, we're not talking about me, are we? Sorry about that. Back to Ben. "It happens to everybody," Dad explained. "All you need is a slump-busting regimen, something to help you 'Reverse the Curse.'"

Ben nodded. "'Reverse the curse' . . . Dad, that's a great idea." He looked down at the band around his left wrist and lit up with the glow of a great idea. "I can move this to the other wrist." He moved it over to his right wrist, and that was only the beginning. "I could wear my clothes backward," he mumbled to himself, pulling his arms through his sleeves and wiggling around until his shirt was facing the other way.

Dad put a hand to his forehead and tried not to laugh. "That's not really what I —"

"Maybe I could talk backward. You are how, Father?" He nodded to himself again, getting more and more excited. It was like he could already feel that mojo flowing back. "Backward walk, can I . . . or, on hands, maybe!"

And that's when my weirdo of a big brother flipped over into a handstand and hand-walked his way out of the store. Backward. "Dad, later you see!"

Dad just stared after him, dumbfounded. "I was thinking not washing your socks for a week would be enough."

But Ben didn't hear him.

Gone already was he.

They say that music soothes the savage beast.

So I brought my guitar over to Scarlett's house the next afternoon to see if it was true.

And you know what? It worked, sort of. For about two minutes, she sat there and listened to me as I sang — it was the quietest two minutes I'd ever spent in her presence.

Hush, little baby, don't say a word,
Mama's gonna buy you a mockingbird. . . .

I should have known it was too good to be true.

"I like your noise!" she screamed, clapping and jumping up and down. I guess she didn't realize that the concert wasn't over.

Except that it was, as soon as she climbed up on the white sofa and started jumping up and down. I had to put down the guitar and stop singing so that I could grab her and pull her back down to ground level. "No, no, you can't jump on the sofa," I reminded her. "You know your daddy wants to keep it clean for when your mommy comes home."

"I want juice!" Scarlett screamed, wriggling out of my grasp and running around the living room in frantic circles.

"Fine." I stomped into the kitchen, wishing that *I* could have a temper tantrum. "But you can only have . . ." I stopped talking as I caught sight of Mary Ferry's magnetic business card on the refrigerator. So she thought I couldn't handle things? I'd show her. I'd show them all. I threw the card in the trash, then pulled a juice box out of the refrigerator. I had a new confidence. After all, I was in middle school. Scarlett was only five. Surely, when we went head-to-head, I would win, right? No five-year-old was going to take me down!

"All right, here's your juice." But before I could hand it to her, my phone rang. "Hey, Geena," I said, when I'd flipped open my little pink cell and put it to my ear. "I can't talk —"

"You need to get to *Juice!* right *now*," she whispered loudly.

Had Geena forgotten that I was a working woman? It's not like I didn't complain about it every chance I got. "I can't."

"Remember who was on the cover of this month's *Teen Scream* magazine? Ashton Kutcher! Well, he's *at* the counter!"

"What?" Oh, my God. Ashton Kutcher was *the* hottest guy in Hollywood. That smile! Those eyes! That awesome, adorable laugh! Geena and I were both totally in love with him. And he was in *Juice!*? Our *Juice!*? And I was . . . somewhere else? Not acceptable. "Are you sure?"

"Positive. You have to get here fast."

"But I'm babysitting." And I wished more than anything that I wasn't. Especially when Scarlett balled up her fists, scrunched up her face, and, in that way that only Scarlett can, exploded, "I! WANT! JUICE!"

"Oh." Geena paused, and I could almost hear her

roll her eyes. "Well, this is pretty much the chance of a lifetime, but okay."

What if Geena was right? What if it really *was* the chance of a lifetime? I mean, wasn't it fate that brought a Hollywood hottie like Ashton Kutcher to my town, to *my* juice bar? And if it *was* fate, then maybe I was meant to run into him. Maybe it was destiny that he would see me and fall instantly, madly in love with me. He would whisk me away with him, back to Hollywood, where we would live a star-studded life of luxury together. I would appear on the cover of every celebrity weekly, and — thanks to my new full-time stylist and personal shopper — I would look fabulous. Maybe it really was my destiny.

I knelt down so that I was facing Scarlett on her level, eye to eye. "Scarlett," I said seriously — so seriously that she instantly stopped screaming, as if she knew I had something super-important to say. "How would you like to go *out* for juice?"

Hey, who was I to argue with destiny?

"Where is he?" I asked breathlessly, sliding into a chair next to Geena. I was holding Scarlett's hand so she wouldn't wander away, but she didn't like it very much. She was all sticky and squirmy, whining about how she wanted juice. But I didn't have time for that now — I had a superstar to meet. I had a destiny to fulfill. "Did I miss him?"

Geena winced and looked away. "Not exactly. It wasn't him."

"What?" Not him? I'd dragged Scarlett out of the house against her father's orders, risked getting fired, and all for nothing? "You told me it was definitely him!"

"It looked exactly like him from behind," Geena protested. "I took a picture of the back of his head with my camera phone. See?"

I grabbed the phone out of Geena's hands. I wanted to throttle her, and that Ashton look-alike whose head was filling her phone's tiny screen. A look-alike who, by the way, didn't look *anything* like the real thing. Even from the back.

"They could be twins," Geena said sadly, shaking her head.

"I want juice!" Scarlett suddenly shouted, oblivious to our misery. She jerked her hand out of mine, as if she couldn't stand to touch someone who wasn't going to deliver on the juice promise. Fine, whatever, I didn't care. I'd just seen my fabulous Hollywood future fall apart before my very eyes. I was crushed. I was frustrated. And, come to think of it . . . I was thirsty.

"I can't believe I came out here for nothing," I complained. "But as long as I'm here, I might as well have a Precious Peach smoothie."

Geena nodded eagerly. She knew that was the best cure for a broken heart — or at least, in this case, a very slightly bruised one. But before I could go place my order, Duane Ogilvy raced over to our table, grinning like he'd just won the lottery.

"Hey, Addie, did you quit?" He held his breath waiting for my answer.

"No." First I was confused — but then, knowing Duane, I began to be a little suspicious. "Why?"

Duane ignored me and turned toward the group of kids who had crowded around our table. "False alarm, everyone!"

That's when the truth sank in. "Is this for your stupid pool?" Unbelievable. As if this wasn't the worst possible time to be reminded of the fact that the whole school thought I was unreliable. Nice to kick me when I'm down, Duane. "For everyone's information, I am *not* going to quit!" I shouted to the crowd, so loudly and angrily that they all took a giant step back. "I can totally handle it."

The grin on Duane's face didn't shrink, not even

a bit. Instead he just arched an eyebrow. "Oh, really?" he asked, in an annoyingly all-knowing tone. "Where's the kid?"

Where else? She was right next to —

Uh-oh.

Scarlett was gone.

My heart rose into my throat and suddenly I felt like I was going to pass out. I'd lost her — I'd lost *Scarlett!* Her father was going to kill me. And then *my* father was going to kill me. I jumped up on my chair to scan the café — surely she couldn't have gone far. Right? *Right?*

I was panicking. My heart was pounding, my head was spinning, I was about to start hyperventilating . . . and that's when I spotted her. She was up at the counter, chugging down a tub-size cup of juice. The sticky red liquid was streaming down her cheeks and chin, and probably getting all over her clothes, but for the moment, I didn't care.

I just cared that I'd found her. I was so relieved that I almost fell off the chair.

I'll never take her out of the apartment again, I promised myself as I went to collect her. Ben was working behind the counter — not that I could see his face. He was still doing the backward, hand-walking thing.

"Cents of fifty and dollars of three will that be," I heard him say — his voice was muffled, probably because his mouth was practically underneath the counter.

I dug through my wallet looking for the right change. I didn't even mind paying for the extra-extra-extra-large juice — all that mattered was getting Scarlett home before anything else went wrong.

And, most important of all — before her father got home!

I'd never been so happy to walk through a door as I was when I finally stepped back into Scarlett's apartment, with Scarlett firmly in hand.

"All right, we've gotta get the berry seeds out of your teeth before your dad gets home," I told her. First order of business was getting her cleaned up. Then I'd figure out how to convince her that she should never, ever tell her dad what she'd been up to this afternoon. Not that I wanted to lie to him or anything. But nothing bad had really happened, right? I mean, okay, so I'd lost Scarlett for about five seconds — but I found her again, and I'd even gotten her that juice she wanted so badly. It had all worked out fine. So I figured he didn't *really* need to know. "Brush your teeth and go to bed."

"I! HATE! BED!"

I rolled my eyes and sank down onto the sofa, totally exhausted. What would it be like, I wondered, to babysit a girl who didn't hate absolutely everything? "You do not hate bed," I countered, knowing it wasn't true. *Just a little longer,* I told myself. I had Scarlett back home, that was the important thing. All I needed to do was clean her, tuck her into bed, wait for her dad to come home, and then I could leave — and forget this whole day had ever happened. If I could just hold out a little longer, if I could just make sure that nothing else went wrong . . .

"Oooooh, I don't feel good," Scarlett suddenly whimpered.

She didn't *look* so good, either. A little pale and green, and she was clutching her stomach, and then —

She exploded. All that juice she'd downed earlier? It all came back up and gushed out of her, spraying everywhere. The juice-colored puke went flying, drenching Scarlett, the rug, the white couch. Me. It was possibly the grossest thing I've ever seen in my entire life. And it was all over me.

"Scarlett!"

"I still don't feel so good," she moaned. And then,

even though it seemed like all the juice in the world had already come out of her, she threw up some more. And then more, until I thought we would drown in it.

And then, just like that, it stopped.

"I feel better now."

Scarlett was smiling. Good for her. So she felt better — and I felt puke-drenched and desperate.

"What am I going to do?" I asked, but I might as well have been asking thin air, because it's not like Scarlett was going to be of any help. She just beamed at me, as if she'd just finished an art project and now she was showing it off.

No, Scarlett couldn't help me. There was only one person who could — and I'd thrown her phone number out in the trash.

But hey, when you're already covered in puke, what's a little garbage? I dug through the trash and pulled out the magnetic business card. And then, even though I didn't want to, even though it's the last thing I had ever wanted to do, I pulled out my cell phone. I dialed the number.

"Hello, Mary?" I could barely get the words out, and for a second, I thought about hanging up. But then I looked around at the neon-puke-colored living room and knew the truth. I was totally and completely out of my league. I sighed and said what had to be said. "I need your help."

Mary Ferry came prepared. When I opened the door to her smug grin, she was towing a giant machine that looked part-vacuum, part-mop, and all lean-mean-cleaning-machine.

"Wow." She peered over my shoulder into the splattered living room. "A class-four puke-storm. I've only seen it once before. And it wasn't this . . . colorful."

"Can you do anything about it?" I was totally stressed. While waiting for Mary to show up, I'd realized that she was my last hope. If she couldn't help me — no one could.

"I can with this baby." Mary pulled the giant cleaning machine into the apartment and displayed it proudly. "I designed it myself. It can clean anything. But it'll cost you."

I sighed. "Whatever it is, I'll pay it."

I don't think Ben's day was going as badly as mine, but it was pretty close. He'd been walking on his hands all day long, and all the blood in his body was rushing to his head, giving him a throbbing headache. And despite all that, he was still trying to be the best *Juice!* employee he could. Or, more to the point, he was trying to be a *better Juice!* employee than the annoying trainee.

"Washed the blenders, I have," he reported to his boss, the muscles in his arms straining as he struggled not to topple over.

"This isn't going to help you get back Employee of the Month," Manager Mike warned him. "In fact, it's creeping me out."

He stalked away, shaking his head as if wondering why he'd hired someone so bizarre in the first place. But Ben wasn't worried. He was certain his plan would work . . . eventually.

"Soon over my slump will be," he told himself confidently.

And then all those hours of walking around upside down finally caught up with him.

And he passed out cold.

In forty-two minutes, Mary had swept through the apartment like a tornado, eliminating every last trace of the neon-colored juice puke. The place looked cleaner than I'd ever seen it. Everything was perfectly in order, the couch was unstained, and the countertops gleamed as brightly as Mary Ferry's unnaturally white teeth.

"Thank you," I gushed. "Really, I don't know how to thank you."

Mary just stuck out her hand.

"Oh. Right." I guess I did know how to thank her. And, I guess in the end, it was worth it. I dug a fat wad of bills out of my pocket and handed them over. "Here." It pained me to see all that money just disappear into Mary's pocket . . . but I didn't have much of a choice.

"Pleasure doing business with you, Addie. Call me anytime."

She rolled her machine toward the door, then paused. She turned back to look at me and wrinkled her nose — which reminded me that there was still one thing left in the apartment that hadn't been washed, buffed, and shined to perfection: me.

"You should change your clothes and wash your hair," Mary recommended. "You're covered in throw-up."

Thanks for the news flash.

Ben had a rescuer, too — and she didn't make him pay.

"You okay?"

Ben woke up to the sound of a sweet, soft voice and opened his eyes. He was staring into the face of a pretty high school junior. She knelt by his side and cradled his head, watching him with deep concern.

"Are you . . . an angel?" Ben asked. He's not great at thinking on his feet — and he's even worse at thinking while flat on his back. But the high-schooler ate it up.

"You're not dead," she giggled. "You just passed out."

"Oh."

"Do you always walk on your hands?"

Ben sat up slowly, cautiously. His head was still pounding — but it felt good to be looking at the world right side up. "Not ever again."

"Careful!" She steadied him — he was still a little wobbly, and he'd sat up too fast. "If this store was making you do this as some kind of stunt, you could sue them." She whipped out a pen and wrote a number across Ben's open palm. "I better give you my phone number, in case you need a witness or something."

A witness. Yeah, right. Ben knew what that meant — he'd caught another girl in his web of charm. It meant his mojo was back — and so was he.

"Back I am!" Ben crowed, shooting a triumphant look at the trainee. Forget this backward stuff, he decided. From now on, it was full steam ahead.

*   *   *

48

By the time Mr. Corn came home, everything in his house was in order, even me. I was still a little wet from the shower, but at least I was clean, dressed, and best of all, didn't smell like throw-up.

"Wow, this place looks fantastic!" he exclaimed.

I relaxed when it became clear he didn't suspect a thing. I guess Mary's full-scale treatment had been worth every penny.

"This sofa looks like it was power-washed," he marveled. "Thank you, Addie. You did a great job. You know what?" He reached into his pocket and pulled out his wallet. "I'm going to give you a bonus." And he counted out some bills — a *lot* of bills — and handed them to me. "And I'm going to refer you to everyone I know!"

"You are?"

"Good babysitters are hard to find." *Not that hard,* I thought. I found one easily enough — all I had to do was dig through the trash and make a phone call. But he kept going before I could say anything. "I know they'll appreciate someone like you, who's responsible."

There was that word again. *Responsible.* It had really hurt that no one had any faith that I could get the job done. No one thought I was responsible. But then, in the end . . . weren't they right? I mean, sure, the apartment was clean, and Scarlett was tucked into bed and asleep. But it's not because I did my job. It's not because I was responsible. I had been a horrible babysitter. I had totally messed up. I hadn't been responsible at all.

But maybe . . . just maybe, it wasn't too late.

"Mr. Corn, I have to tell you something." I paused and looked down at the wad of cash in my hand, enjoying the way it felt. I had a feeling that I wouldn't be holding it for much longer. "You know that list of instructions you gave me? Well, there's something you should know. . . ."

When I walked into *Juice!* that night, no one was happier to see me than Duane Ogilvy. He knew exactly what my presence meant.

"We got a time, people!" he shouted as I walked in the door. I tried my best to ignore him — Geena was wailing for me, and all I wanted to do was sit down at our familiar table, order a familiar drink, and forget the whole babysitting thing had ever happened. It just wasn't meant to be. "She quit! Six-twenty-seven! Who had six-twenty-seven on the twenty-third?" No answer. "Six-twenty-seven? Anybody?"

As Duane wandered off to find the winner of his stupid pool, Geena patted me on the shoulder sympathetically. "I shouldn't have called you with that bogus hottie sighting."

True, but . . . "It's not your fault," I admitted. "I

guess I'm not cut out for the high-powered world of professional babysitting. Maybe sometimes the responsible thing to do is quit."

"You're right. It's important to know your limits. I mean, I can't date guys who are shorter than me —"

Fortunately, Zach joined us before Geena could elaborate any more on her "limits." "I heard the news," he said, sitting down.

"Sorry." After all, Zach was the real loser here — that cash I'd handed back was supposed to be his. "But I swear I'll pay you back. Eventually."

Zach shrugged and gave me a mysterious smile. "Don't worry. We're cool."

He pulled out a wad of cash, a big one, and handed half of it to Geena. What was the deal?

"We won Duane Ogilvy's pool," Zach explained. "Consider yourself paid off."

"You guys bet against me?" Unbelievable! My own best friends, rooting for me to fail? Though . . . I guess I couldn't blame them, considering that they'd been right.

"You gotta do what you gotta do," Zach said, shrugging again. "Wanna borrow some money for a juice?"

"Nope. I've learned my lesson. I'm not gonna

borrow anything ever again. In fact, I have a job interview tomorrow."

"Where?" they chorused, exchanging surprised
looks. They probably thought I was jumping back into
the working world a little too fast — or maybe they figured I'd just fail all over again.

Not this time. I'd finally found the perfect job for
me, something I couldn't mess up. I just had to make it
past the interview. And something told me that wouldn't
be a problem. . . .

"I'm very responsible," I told my interviewer,
standing up as straight and tall as I possibly could. *How
do you* look *responsible*? I wondered, and hoped that it
had something to do with posture. "I'm a hard worker,
and retail is my passion." I slid a sheet of paper across
the counter to the store's manager. "Here's my résumé.
I have excellent references."

"Sue and Nancy Singer," he read aloud, and
grinned. Now he knew he'd have to hire me — after all,
my two references were his wife and his dog! But Dad
kept a stern look on his face. "I see a number for Sue,
but do you have a way to contact this 'Nancy'?"

"Daaaaad!" I protested. How long was this fake
interview going to last before he let me have the job?

"All right, all right. Can you start now?"

"Totally!" Finally, a *real* job — and one that didn't involve *any* wild, screaming five-year-olds. Dad handed me a Singer Sporting Goods polo shirt, and I pulled it on over my T-shirt. I'd never felt so official, so important.

"Thanks, Dad."

"Here's your first duty."

My first duty. See, didn't that sound important? I loved to think that suddenly I was a crucial element in the success of Singer Sporting Goods. Having a job — a real job — was so glamorous!

Dad plunked a pair of roller skates on the counter. "Tightening the wheels on roller skates," he explained.

Um, okay, so it wasn't *that* glamorous.

He handed me a tiny screwdriver. "Remember, righty tighty, lefty loosey!"

So maybe it wasn't the most exciting job in the world, but it was a job, and that meant a paycheck. And *that* meant plenty of fruit smoothies and cool earrings from the mall.

I got busy tightening those roller skates while Dad answered the phone. "Singer Sporting Goods. Oh, hey, Ashton."

Did he just say Ashton?

I shook my head. It couldn't be, you know, *that*

Ashton. I was through jumping to conclusions and getting distracted from my responsibilities, remember? For
me, it was all about the roller skates. Even if it was possible my dad was on the phone with . . .

What was I thinking. My dad? No way. Couldn't be.

"I've got your order right here," Dad continued.
"You can pick it up anytime. Great, see you anytime."

"Who was that?" I asked casually, once he'd hung
up. Not because I was curious, of course. I was just being
polite. Really.

"A customer. He's coming in to pick up this whiffleball he ordered."

Dad showed me the receipt.

My eyes bugged out of my head. My jaw dropped
open. Because there it was. Right under the Singer
Sporting Goods logo, right under the whiffleball order.
His name. *Ashton. Kutcher.*

"Ashton Kutcher?" I whispered. Suddenly, I didn't
have enough breath in me to speak out loud. He's coming *here*?"

"Yeah." Dad looked confused. "You know him?"

So my tale of poverty and woe had a *very* happy
ending. I was shocked when I found out that Ashton
Kutcher was one of Dad's regular customers — but not

nearly as shocked as Geena was when she opened up the photo I e-mailed her. There I was, standing right next to Ashton, both of us wearing Singer Sporting Goods T-shirts. I just wish I could have been there to see the look on Geena's face — even when I did see her, hours later, she was still pale and bug-eyed. I know I'd blown her mind.

Ashton was really nice and totally cool about taking the picture with me — and yes, he's just as cute in person. And taller.

That night I went home after a hard day's work, feeling pretty good about myself. After all, I had a job, a picture of myself with a major Hollywood star — and soon I'd even have a paycheck. I went straight upstairs to find my guitar, because there was a song that had been bouncing around my head for hours and I needed to get it out.

I finally got a job and can you believe
My dad was the only one who would hire me.
Before I got puked on,
But learned responsibility.
Now I've got a picture of Ashton and me.
Yeah, I got a picture of Ashton and me!

Have you ever noticed that just when you've finally gotten things worked out in one area of your life, another area pretty much blows up in your face? Like, just when you've finally figured out algebra, you realize you totally forgot to study for that Shakespeare test? Or just when you've convinced your mom not to ground you for missing curfew, your dad grounds you for forgetting to clean out the garage?

It's a fact of life, I guess. Or at least, it's a fact of *my life.*

See, just when I'd gotten the whole money thing straightened out — *just* when I'd started to relax and think that I had my life pretty much in order — that's when it happened. That's when I had a total meltdown. We're talking out of control, losing it, all-systems failure. Trust me, it wasn't pretty.

And it wasn't about the job thing at all — no, the problem actually came from the last place I expected. It came from the one thing in my life that I thought I'd finally taken care of, that wouldn't cause me any problems ever again.

It came from my boyfriend. Randy Klein.

Here's the thing. Not having a boyfriend? That was no fun at all. Especially the part where I had a huge crush on Jake Behari — every time I saw him in the halls, I wanted to melt. And every time I saw him walking down the hall with his *girlfriend*, it felt like he was ripping my heart out, over and over again. Sure, they broke up eventually, but it didn't matter — because by that time, I had discovered Randy Klein. And you know what? I'd gotten a crush on *him*! But this time there was a big difference: Randy liked me, too. Can you believe it? And suddenly, the whole crush thing wasn't making me so miserable after all. It was a little scary, and then it was a little exciting — but you want to know the weird thing? Once Randy and I started hanging out together a lot, the whole thing started to seem pretty normal. Suddenly, I was dating a boy, and it seemed like the most natural thing in the world. The best part was that I could stop stressing about it. I could stop worrying about whether someone liked me or whether he would figure out if I liked him. I could just enjoy myself, and I could enjoy hanging out with Randy.

It's sort of like what I was saying before about money, and how it seems like with all the money in the world, you could solve all your problems. It's kind of the same thing with a boyfriend, right? When you *don't* have one, it can seem like the biggest problem in the world — and you think that if you could just get a boy to like you, all your problems would be solved.

That's what I thought, at least.

Boy, was I wrong.

Let me paint a mental image for you. Randy Klein, huddled over a tiny table in a small, dark room illuminated by a single bare lightbulb hanging from the ceiling. He's nervous, jittery — you can tell because his eyes keep darting back and forth, never landing on one spot for too long. His left leg won't stop bouncing up and down. Beads of sweat are forming on his brow, trickling down the side of his face. He doesn't even notice. He's too focused on his interrogator, the dark, shadowy figure who has become the center of his narrow world. The figure won't give up, won't stop asking question after question after question until he's so beaten down he'll tell the whole truth and nothing but the truth.

The figure won't stop until he doesn't have the strength to lie.

The figure, of course, was me.

"Where were you?" I asked him, pacing back and forth as he fumbled and fidgeted at his table. Hopefully, he felt that the walls were closing in. I knew *I* was closing in . . . on the truth.

"I told you, I was at swim practice."

"Practice ends at three," I spit out. I had all the facts at my fingertips. You had to, in this business. "You didn't show up until three-seventeen. It doesn't take seventeen minutes to get from the pool to the lockers."

"I . . . I might've stopped for a drink of water —"

What was that? A hesitation? *Not* acceptable. *"Might've?"* I pounced. "Did you or didn't you?"

"I did!"

That's when I pulled out all the stops. I flicked on the spotlight, and Randy flinched under the harsh white beam, squinting into the light. Now the sweat was pouring down him. It's hot under the harsh light of truth, isn't it, Randy?

I moved in for the kill.

"Who were you with?"

"No one! I was by myself." Ha! A likely story.

"And you didn't talk to anyone?"

"Uh, I think I said hi to Nick and Tom —"

I slammed my hands down on the table with a sharp bang, and he jumped back. But he couldn't escape, not from me.

"I called you six times! Why didn't you answer your cell phone?"

"I didn't hear it," he sobbed. "It was on vibrate!"

Now that he'd finally broken down, I knew I would get to the *real* story and solve this crime —

Okay, okay, so there was no interrogation room and no spotlight, it was all in my imagination. But there was an interrogation — even if it took place in the middle of the school hallway, by our lockers — and Randy was definitely nervous. And I was pretty sure that one thing wasn't in my imagination: his crime. I just needed to press a little more and I was sure I'd squeeze it out of him.

"I told you not to put your phone on vibrate so you can always hear my signature ring!" I complained.

"I'm sorry I'm, like, seven minutes late or whatever."

Sorry wouldn't cut it. Not if he was where I thought he was. The time for subtlety was over. I'd just have to come right out and ask. "Are you in love with Patti Perez?"

"What? Okay, you're acting crazy." And maybe I

was . . . crazy like a fox! I knew he was hiding something. I just knew it. "I'll just . . . talk to you later."

Notice how he didn't answer me? Notice how he'd just walked away? I wasn't going to let him get away with that.

"Or is it Mary Ferry?" I shrieked after him. "I've seen the way you look at each other!"

Um, yeah. So that was a low point in my relationship with Randy Klein, as maybe you've already guessed.

"Stop shouting, Singer," Principal Brandywine snapped, driving by me on her little motorized scooter. "This is a place of learning, not a hog-calling contest at the county rodeo."

"It's Principal Brandywine," I gasped, suddenly sure of it. "He's seeing P-Bran behind my back. She doesn't need that scooter, you know!" I shouted after Randy, even though he'd long since disappeared down the hall. "She's just lazy!"

And *that* was an even lower point in my relationship with Randy.

You may be asking yourself, "How did a perfectly sane and normal girl like Addie Singer sink so low?" It's a *long* story — but it's one you should pay close attention to. After all, some day, it could happen to you. . . .

When it all started, things were great. In fact, they couldn't have been better. I had great friends, I was doing well in school, I was writing a lot of awesome new songs, and best of all, I had a boyfriend who's, well, totally hot. Nothing could possibly be bad, right?

Wrong.

There I was in the girls' bathroom with Geena, playing with our hairstyles in front of the big wall-length mirror.

"Do you think I could pull off cornrows?" I asked, pulling my hair tight against my head to try to imagine what it might look like.

Geena rolled her eyes. "Have you ever seen white girls with cornrows? Their heads look like giant Hacky Sacks."

In other words, it was just a typical morning for us, the start of another great day. Or so I thought. That's when Cranberry St. Clare and Maris Bingham walked into the bathroom. Always a bad sign. And the fact that they came in with Patti Perez? Not encouraging. Patti was one of the popular girls at school. And, did I mention, the most snotty girl in the world? I should have known that the day was about to take a significant turn for the worse.

"... so I was totally thinking, 'Go ahead, honey,'" Cranberry was saying, "'you can walk in front of me anytime!'"

Maris laughed and nodded, her silky-smooth blond hair bouncing up and down. "He's in my history class and every day I'm, like, please let him get called to the board so I can stare at —"

"Eye-Candy Randy Klein!" The three of them giggled in unison. And then they spotted me — and they fell silent, *fast*. So fast that you could almost hear the sound of brakes screeching as they stopped in their tracks, shut their mouths, and froze.

"Eye-Candy Randy Klein?" I asked slowly, staring Patti down.

Geena, who gets a little ... excited in situations like this, dropped her lip gloss on the counter and pounded her fist into her hand. "Okay, it's go-time." She began pulling out her earrings. "Someone hold my jewelry —"

But I didn't need her to protect me. I didn't need anyone to protect me. From what? Patti and her minions? Puh-leeze. "How funny!" I forced a smile, then a laugh, hoping it didn't sound too fake. "Eye-Candy Randy. I've never heard that before!"

In unison, Patti, Maris, and Cranberry sighed with relief, and Geena put her earrings back in.

"Uh, yeah," Patti mumbled, still a little wary. "Some of the girls have, kind of, given Randy that nickname."

"I like it," I told her, trying to convince myself that it was true. "It's cute."

"So you're, like, totally cool with it?" Maris asked incredulously.

I shrugged. "Sure. I trust Randy. Besides, that kind of thing comes with the territory when you're dating the cutest boy in seventh grade."

Geena looked at me like I was crazy, and Maris, Cranberry, and Patti looked . . . impressed? I couldn't be sure, because I'd never seen that expression on their faces before.

As we walked out of the bathroom, Geena paused and glared at the three of them. "Just so you know, I don't roll like that. When I get a boyfriend, you better not come up with any cutesy nicknames for him."

Cranberry sneered. "By the time *you* get a boyfriend, we'll be too old to think of any."

"Burn!" Maris and Cranberry cheered, tapping their fingers together the way they always do, as if they're too cool to just slap each other five.

Geena shook her head, sighed, and began removing her earrings again. Uh-oh. "Yeah, it's go-time."

Geena was right — sort of. I pulled her through

65

the bathroom door before she really got into fight mode and past the point of no return. It was most definitely time for us to go.

If my school day had started out like normal, things at home were anything but. My parents had decided to build an extension on the house, and that meant chaos. Lots of it. That week, they were interviewing contractors — they needed to find someone who could take control of all the construction and design and, basically, put our house in order. And in Jason, a guy in his mid-twenties who'd just moved to town, they were pretty sure they'd found exactly what they needed.

"We've both started doing a lot of work out of the house," Mom explained as Jason took notes on his clipboard.

"Yeah. Work, work, work, work . . . workity-work, work," Dad added. *Trying* to help.

"Don't feel you have to chime in," Mom whispered to him. She likes to be in control of business negotiations. And I think you can see why. She turned back to Jason and smiled like nothing had just happened. "Anyway, we want to build an addition off the kitchen that we could use as a home office slash guest bedroom. You know, for when my mother comes to stay —"

"Your mother is coming to stay?" Dad's eyes widened in horror.

"No, I'm just using that as an example. But yeah, probably."

"Sure, Mr. and Mrs. Singer," Jason said quickly, before things could go any further. See? I told you he was perfect. "That shouldn't be a problem. Let me see if I can give you an estimate now."

Dad waved Mom down, his silent way of telling her that *he* would handle this part of the negotiation. He put his hands on his hips and started rocking gently back and forth. It's Dad's way of looking like a tough guy. "Now, we don't want to spend a lot of money," he warned gruffly.

"It should be pretty inexpensive." He scribbled a number on his clipboard and showed it to Dad. "How does this work for you?"

When Dad looked back up at Jason, his tough expression was gone, replaced by the starry eyes of a man in love . . . with a bargain. My father's never met a discount, sale, coupon, or outlet store marked-down defective merchandise that he didn't adore, and Jason's rock-bottom construction pricing was no different. It was love at first sight.

"Are you thirsty, Jason?" Dad asked, rushing over

to the cabinet to pull out a glass. "Can I get you anything? Sparkling water with lemon?"

That's my dad. Give him a discount and you'll be his friend for life.

"Wow, that sounds great," Mom told Jason, much more calmly. "Now I know why you come so highly recommended."

Jason smiled, and a faint pink color bloomed in his cheeks.

"Are you blushing?" Dad asked. He turned to Mom. "Is he blushing?"

"Thanks, Mrs. Singer," Jason said, and now the faint pink had darkened into a bright tomato red. "That's good to know. I just recently moved here from Ohio, and it's been a little tough."

"You're kidding — Jeff and I have family in Ohio!" Mom exclaimed.

"It was a scary decision to leave. . . . I tell you, most nights, I get really homesick."

Remember how much my dad loves saving money? Well, multiply that by about a thousand, and you'll get the amount that my mom loves mothering people.

"Awww," she sighed at the thought of Jason sitting home at nights missing Ohio. And when she looked at him, she didn't see a potential contractor — she saw a lost little boy that she could save. She'd just have to hire him first!

That afternoon, Randy and I met up with Zach at *Juice!* He was hanging out with some of his buddies from the basketball team, and when I got there, they were all huddled over a big cardboard box, oohing and ahhing. When I got closer, I realized that box was filled with little stuffed bullfrogs, each dressed in a Rocky Road Middle School basketball uniform. Bizarre.

I mean, don't get me wrong — they *were* adorable. But still bizarre.

"What do you guys think?" Zach asked, picking up one of the bullfrogs and making it do a little dance on top of the cardboard box. "Pretty sweet, right?"

"We're gonna sell 'em at the games to raise money for a new team van," his friend Archie explained.

"What happened to the old van?" I asked, picking up one of the stuffed bullfrogs and cradling it in the palm of my hand. So cute.

"We were sharing one with the local prison," Zach said. "There was a jailbreak. . . ."

"Two dudes hot-wired it and took off for Canada," Archie finished mournfully.

Zach sighed. "Yeah, and I left my gym bag in the

back. Some guy in Nova Scotia is whale-watching in my *Save the Last Dance* T-shirt."

Uh, hello, can we say chick flick?

"What?" Zach asked indignantly when he saw the looks we were giving him. "I loved that movie."

Normally, I would have started teasing Zach about his bizarro love for dance movies, but I got distracted by the looks these two girls gave us as they were passing by. Or more specifically, the looks they gave *Randy*. They whispered and giggled to each other. But I knew what they were thinking: *Eye-Candy Randy*. And it burned me up.

"Razz-mataz and a Berry Bomber," the girl up at the counter called.

"That's us," Randy said, holding up our drink ticket. "I'll get it."

I watched him as he walked to the counter — he was so totally adorable, it was true. And that made me really happy. For about ten seconds. Because then I realized that I wasn't the only one in *Juice!* who was noticing Randy's cute walk and the hot way his hair bounced up and down as he walked. In fact, it seemed like every girl in the place had stopped talking and turned to gaze at him. At *my* boyfriend.

It's cool, I told myself, even though it didn't feel

cool. *Totally cool.* Comes with the territory, right? Like I told Maris and Cranberry, that's what you get for dating the cutest boy in seventh grade. Let them stare — it didn't *mean* anything. Right?

"Don't worry about it," the girl at the counter said when Randy pulled out his wallet to pay for the smoothies. She waved away his money. "It's on the house."

"Really?" Randy smiled, and even from halfway across the room I could see the little dimples that appeared when he grinned. I love those dimples.

"Totally. Your cute smile is payment enough."

Excuse me? That cute smile was *my* cute smile! Those dimples were *my* cute dimples. They weren't for some random *Juice!* trainee to appreciate. Who was she, trying to buy his affection?

I wouldn't let it bother me, though. I would stay calm. I would stay cool. No sir, I didn't care if every girl in the place was checking out my boyfriend, that wasn't my problem. I was above all that —

"Addie. Addie!" Zach yelled, trying to grab the bullfrog out of my hands. "You're choking Roger!" And he was right. I'd almost popped the head off of the poor bullfrog. Guess I wasn't so cool after all.

But could you blame me? I mean, as if the girl up at the counter wasn't bad enough, I had to put up with

Patti Perez at the next table. I'm guessing she didn't know I was there.

"How could Eye-Candy Randy be with Average-Addie Singer when *I'm* available?" she asked Maris and Cranberry, who shook their heads wildly. So wildly that they caught sight of me. Maris jerked her head in my direction — and Patti, when she saw me, at least had the grace to look a little embarrassed.

"Oh, hey, Average," Patti said, giving me an icy smile. "Cute pants." I said a *little* embarrassed. Guess it passed quickly. She glanced up as Randy came back toward our table. "Almost as cute as Randy."

I didn't say anything back to Patti. I didn't say anything to anyone. I just squeezed that bullfrog tighter and tighter as my blood began to boil. I took a deep breath in, held it for a second, then blew all my air out at once. I felt like steam should be coming out of my ears. But still, all I did was hold that bullfrog tighter and tighter, until my knuckles turned white. I squeezed and squeezed and squeezed . . . and then I snapped! I ripped the head off the bullfrog and threw it across the room as white stuffing exploded all over the table.

"Uh, okay," Zach said, gently pulling the remains of Roger the bullfrog out of my hands. Poor Roger. He hadn't done anything. It's not like *he* wanted to steal my boyfriend. Not like *every girl in school*! "That'll be four dollars and fifty cents."

Archie put a protective arm around the box of bullfrogs and pulled it across the table, out of my reach. "We pretty much have a 'you pull the head off it, you buy it' policy."

That night at dinner, everything seemed a little off. I was still obsessing over Randy, of course. And my parents? Well, they were obsessing over their new best friend and surrogate son, Jason.

"So Rick Neederhorn thought he had me pinned, right," Ben was saying, telling yet another one of his endless wrestling stories. He does it every night during wrestling season — but this night, there was one big difference. Mom and Dad weren't hanging on his every boring word. In fact, they didn't seem to be listening at all.

"Oh, Jason called," Mom told Dad. "He's going to start building the addition tomorrow! You guys are gonna love him," she assured us. As if she hadn't already done so about twenty times since the beginning of dinner.

"He just moved here from Ohio and opened his own contracting company —" Dad began.

"So anyway, just before the count, I pulled out my

signature half nelson," Ben interrupted, ignoring them as stubbornly as they were ignoring him.

"Even though he looks like he's about sixteen years old," Mom added, smiling sweetly as if she thought Jason looked more like a lost puppy than a sixteen-year-old contractor.

"He skipped second grade and graduated high school early," Dad boasted.

Ben threw down his fork. "Are you guys listening at all?"

"I wonder if Jason likes pumpkin bread," Mom mused, as if her darling son had never spoken. "I'll go to the store tomorrow —"

"Oh, yeah?" Ben said loudly. "Well, does 'Jason the Wonderful' always carry two guns?" Ben lifted up his arm and flexed his biceps, nodding proudly. "Yeah, that's right. Locked" — he jerked his head toward his right bicep — "and loaded." He gestured toward his left. "Twenty-eight-inch python barrels."

Have I mentioned that in times of stress, my brother gets even weirder than usual?

I guess maybe you figured that out already.

Fortunately, even though my parents seemed to have forgotten that Ben existed, they still remembered me. And just like she always does, Mom picked up on the fact that things in my life weren't quite right.

"Addie, honey, you've been awfully quiet," she said suddenly. "Everything okay?"

Ben was still muttering to himself. "I bet *Jason* doesn't know anything about weight lifting."

I ignored him. It felt good. "Yeah, I guess," I told Mom. But then I reconsidered. After all, once in a very great while, parents actually give you good advice, right? So maybe this would be one of those times. "Actually, no. The girls in school have nicknamed Randy 'Eye-Candy Randy.'"

"Nice." Ben grinned. "My nickname was 'Ben the Hottie.'"

"Not talking about you. No one cares," I snapped. "I don't know, Mom, I guess I never noticed before the way other girls looked at Randy."

Mom pursed her lips. "Addie, you have nothing to worry about," she assured me. "Randy adores you."

"I know, but I can't help it. I feel . . . kinda jealous." It was the first time I'd said it out loud. You would think that admitting it might have made me feel better — but the weird thing was, saying the word just made me feel even *more* jealous. Like I wanted to call

Randy right that instant so I could make sure I knew exactly what he was doing and who he was with.

"Jealousy isn't pretty," Mom warned, and I wondered if she could tell what I was thinking. "That's why they call it the green-eyed monster."

"Listen to your mom, she knows," Dad added. Uh-oh. Dad's take on my love life is never particularly . . . useful. Or sane. "When we started dating, other girls would throw themselves at me all the time and she would get *so* jealous."

Mom burst into laughter, throwing her head back and chuckling so hard it seemed for a second like she might fall off her chair. Then she caught Dad's wounded stare. "I'm sorry," she said quickly. "I thought you were kidding."

After that, nothing was quite the same. Sure, everything *looked* the same — Randy still walked down the hall holding my hand, he still came to meet me after class, he still bought me smoothies. But it didn't *feel* the same. It didn't make me happy. Because wherever we were, whatever we were doing, I only had one thought on my mind: the competition. All those other girls who thought Randy was the cutest thing they'd ever seen — all those girls who wanted to steal him away.

"Walk in front of me," I said suddenly as Randy and I were walking down the hall. I pulled my hand out of his and pushed him ahead of me.

"What? Why?"

"No reason," I lied. "Just for fun." I glared at the girls who were walking alongside us. Let them just try to stare at Randy now that I was in the way, blocking their loving gazes.

"Hey, eyes front, Cranberry!" I ordered as she walked past us and checked him out. You couldn't sneak anything past me.

"What're you giggling about?" I snapped as we walked past a giggling group of cheerleaders. Their smiles dropped off their faces as soon as they heard my voice. "Put a sock in it, Lisa."

But the halls were filled with girls — every time I stopped one potential boyfriend thief, another popped up in her place. Next up was Mary Ferry. Sure, she was *supposedly* dating Duane Ogilvy. But I knew better — who would want Duane when they could have Randy? She smiled shyly at him as we passed, and I exploded.

"Stop checking out my boyfriend, Mary Ferry!" I yelled.

Mary ran away, and Randy stopped walking. He looked me in the eye, as if trying to figure out what was going on inside my head. "Addie, what's going on? You're acting really weird."

"I'm just letting these girls know what's up."

But like I say, just when you think you've got one problem taken care of, another one sprouts up in its place. I might have succeeded in scaring off some of the girls, but obviously not all of them. When Randy and I started walking again and made it to our lockers, I almost screamed. Because someone had spray-painted graffiti on one of the lockers just down the hall from us: GIMME A PIECE OF EYE-CANDY RANDY!

"Principal Brandywine!" I yelled, totally freaking out. The enemy was everywhere! "Can we please get some paintbrushes and cover up this filth?"

Randy was backing away from me, and that adorable smile was nowhere to be seen. But I was too angry to even notice. "Uh, gotta go to class," he mumbled. "See you later."

"Yeah, you will!" I said determinedly. And, just in case there was anyone left in the halls who didn't get that Randy was *my* boyfriend and would see *me* later, I repeated myself, loud and clear. "Yeah! He *will*!"

What happened next? Well, it's all kind of jumbled together in my head. With every passing moment I was more and more obsessed with protecting Randy from other girls. And with all that fear and jealousy bouncing around in my brain, I didn't have the energy to keep track of anything else that was going on. My world had narrowed to a single person: Randy. Wherever he went, I followed.

Maybe you'll understand better if you hear the song I wrote. I should warn you ahead of time, it's kind of embarrassing. But like I say, I was in the early stages of total meltdown, so embarrassment was pretty much guaranteed.

Back off, sister, you better back off.
I don't like what you're thinking of.

That's what I was singing in my head when I snuck up on Randy after his math class, grabbed his hand, and pulled him away. The nerve of him, talking to *girls* — I knew what they were thinking.

You can look, but you can't touch.
No, don't even look, 'cause that's too much.
Don't think twice. I'm everywhere.

The lyrics floated through my head as I stalked him in the cafeteria, finally catching him having lunch with a bunch of his friends. Some of them *girls*. I don't think so. I plopped myself down on the overcrowded bench, squeezing him over to make room for me — some kid on the other side fell off with a loud thud. But I didn't care. I just cared about throwing my arm around Randy's shoulder so that everyone would know *he* was with *me*.

Even when he's in the dentist chair.
Is that hygienist looking at his derriere?

I wrote those lines while he was getting his teeth cleaned. I came with him and held his hand, making sure I stayed between him and the hygienist. Hey, I said the song was *embarrassing*, I never said *creative* — or *sane*.

Basically, it all boiled down to one simple message, broadcast to every girl in the world who wasn't me:

Back off, sister.
Back OFF!

And finally, even Randy started to notice that something a little strange was going on.

"Where have you been?" I asked as soon as he came into sight. I'd been waiting at my locker for an eternity, checking my watch, tapping my foot, wondering what kind of trouble he could have gotten into on his way from the pool. *Girl* trouble. I was sure of it.

"What're you talking about?" He stared at me in

wide-eyed confusion. "I said I'd meet you here after practice."

He smiled a dopey little smile, but I wasn't about to be distracted. I wanted to get to the bottom of this. "Yeah, and your practice ended seventeen minutes ago. It doesn't take seventeen minutes to get from the pool to the lockers, Randy." It would only take that long if — I gasped. "Unless you stopped to talk to someone on the way. Did you? Did you stop to talk to someone?"

But before he could answer, Maris walked by. She smiled at us both. But I knew she only had eyes for Randy. *Eye-Candy Randy*, remember?

I felt my blood boiling again, and in my imagination, everything changed. My eyes started to glow green, like I'd turned into an avenging monster filled with jealous rage. In my imagination, I leaped onto Maris and tackled her to the ground. Then I picked her up like a sack of potatoes.

"Addie, no! Stop!" Imaginary Randy pleaded. *Of course* he wanted me to stop. He didn't want me to hurt the girl he was probably cheating on me with, right?

And in my imagination I ripped the door off a locker with the strength of the Incredible Hulk, then I shoved Maris inside.

"Addie. Addie!" Randy shouted — loud enough

that it broke through my fantasy. Maris had walked safely past us. The door to the locker was still intact. My eyes weren't glowing green. But Randy was pretty sure something was going on. Maybe I was lucky he didn't know what. "You've been acting so weird lately . . . what's going on with you?"

"Oh, wouldn't you like to know?" I said suspiciously. If he knew I was onto him, that would just make it all the easier for him to sneak around. "Why don't you just ask Maris if you're so curious?"

"What? That doesn't even make any sense."

In my head, the glowing green eyes were back. So was the incredible strength. And the incredible jealousy. "I don't have to make sense!" I roared. "I'm your *girlfriend*!"

I was sitting at my desk doing an important search on my laptop when Geena and Zach walked in. I ignored them. I was too busy with the all-important task at hand. Maybe you can guess what it was. They did.

"Hi, Addie," Geena said, as they came into my bedroom.

Zach peered over my shoulder to catch a glimpse of the laptop screen. "Uh-oh. She's googling Randy Klein."

"Did you know Randy was in a *coed* 4-H club when he was in third grade?" I asked indignantly. "What little floozy was he raising sheep with?!"

"I'm sorry, Addie," Zach said, reaching over me. "This is for your own good." He pulled out my Ethernet cable with a dramatic flourish. I kept typing.

Welcome to the twenty-first century, Zach. "Wireless Internet," I pointed out, only half paying attention — I'd just discovered a link to Randy Klein's kindergarten swim team. *Coed!* Just imagine him strutting around in a bathing suit in front of all those girls.

That's when Geena slammed the laptop shut. "This has got to stop. I thought you said you trusted Randy!"

"I do trust him. . . ." Well, sort of. "It's everyone else I'm worried about!"

Zach turned me around in my chair and forced me to look him in the eye. "If you don't get your jealousy under control, you're going to drive him away," he warned.

"You don't want to lose Randy, do you?" Geena warned.

I hated to agree with them, but . . .

"No," I admitted.

"Good." Zach gave Geena a nod, and she pulled a

pamphlet out of her bag. "According to this, admitting that you're jealous is the first step."

Geena handed the pamphlet to me.

"How to Make Your Own Boots?" I read in confusion.

Geena grabbed the pamphlet back and stuffed it into her bag. Then she pulled out another one. "Wrong pamphlet. Here."

"Five Steps to Overcoming Jealousy," I read. Well, that made more sense at least. But I still didn't like the sound of this.

Zach knelt in front of me and in his dramatic, after-school special voice, intoned, "We'll help you beat this!"

They meant well. But I was pretty sure it was going to take more than a pamphlet to defeat the not-so-jolly green giant who was living inside of me. But maybe there was hope. After all, like Zach had said, I'd taken the first step. And it was a snap. So how tough could the other four be?

We started the next day, at lunch.

"Okay, 'Step Two,'" Geena read from the pamphlet. "'Isolate the Cause of the Jealousy.'"

See, what did I tell you? This was going to be a snap.

"That's easy," I boasted. "All the girls who flirt with Randy in school, at *Juice!*" I could feel the green monster stirring inside of me, more and more eager to come out as I thought of all the girls who just lay in wait for poor, innocent Randy to cross their paths. "At the mall, on the street, wherever we go, they're always there, like cockroaches —"

A wave of icy water washed over me, and I stopped, too shocked to speak. Zach had thrown his water in my face. Now, why would my best friend do something like that?

"Well, I had to do *something*," Zach defended himself as Geena gave him the same accusing stare I had on my face. "She was getting hysterical."

I wiped my drenched bangs off my face as Geena put a gentle hand on my shoulder.

"Addie, those girls aren't the cause, they're a symptom," she explained. "*You're* the cause."

"Me?" Now she was making even less sense than Zach.

"You think because all these girls flirt with Randy, he might find someone he likes better than you. Your *insecurity* is the cause of your jealousy, not the girls."

"Well, I wouldn't *have* any insecurity if it weren't for the girls —"

For that, I got another cupful of water in my face.

"Right," I said, mopping myself off. I knew when I was beat. "My insecurity is the cause of my jealousy." Geena and Zach looked so proud and pleased, as if I'd given them a special present. Well, maybe now they could give me something special. I squinted through the water that was still pouring down my face. "So, um, can you get me a paper towel or something?"

Step Three was "Eliminating One Jealousy Trigger," and I knew exactly what I wanted to eliminate. The middle stall in the girls' bathroom had some unsightly graffiti that definitely needed taking care of.

EYE-CANDY RANDY!

I'd fix that. Step Three, right? I pulled out a tube of lip gloss and turned the exclamation point into a plus sign. Then I added my name. Now the stall read:

EYE-CANDY RANDY + ADDIE SINGER

I drew a big heart around the whole thing and smiled, proud of myself. Now everyone would know: You can look, but you can't touch.

I was so proud of myself that I didn't even mind when Principal Brandywine motored up, a pink detention slip already in hand. She slipped it to me without even pausing, and I took it from her without even looking. It was no more than I'd expected.

And you know what?

Totally worth it.

Step Four: "Apologize to Someone You May Have Hurt Due to Your Jealousy."

I guess I could have apologized to Maris or Cranberry — but somehow, Mary Ferry seemed a much easier choice. I found her at her locker.

"Hi, Mary Ferry," I said cheerfully.

She jumped back as soon as she saw me, slammed

her locker door, and looked ready to run. "I wasn't looking at your boyfriend!"

"Sorry about that. Here." I handed her a fuzzy pen with a red bow tied around it and a sheet of stickers. "Please accept these as an apology."

Mary frowned. "I don't know, Addie. You really hurt my feelings —" Then she took a closer look at the stickers, and her face lit up. "Puffalumps!"

And finally, I was ready for Step Five. According to the pamphlet, that meant "Building Up Your Self-Esteem." And the pamphlet told me exactly how to do it. "Remember, insecurity causes jealousy, so take time out to tell yourself all the good, positive things people like about you."

How bad could that be?

So as soon as I got home that day, I locked myself in the bathroom and stared at myself in the mirror. "You're nice," I told myself. "You're smart. You're funny. You're talented."

"You're talking to yourself in the mirror!" Ben shouted from the other side of the door. "Quit hogging the bathroom, freak!"

The pamphlet didn't say anything about ignoring jerky older brothers who tried to ruin your self-esteem by calling you a freak. And it didn't mention that when that happened, you should stay in the bathroom for an extra hour, just to punish him.

But I'm sure the pamphlet would have approved.

While I was trying to rebuild my sanity, Mom and Dad were busy rebuilding the house. Or at least, they were watching *Jason* build, and they were loving it. Ben? Not so much.

"Jason, I'm amazed at how much you've built already!" Mom exclaimed, once Jason finished giving them a tour of the half-built addition.

"Aw, it's nothing, Mrs. Singer." He helped her through the white plastic curtain separating the new extension from our old kitchen. "Just want to do a good job and get out of your hair."

"What's your rush?" Dad asked quickly. "Hey, you like board games? 'Cause we've got plenty of board games."

Jason shook his head. "I better get back to work. After all, I am on the clock."

Ben, who had wandered into the kitchen, lugging a big, clunky thing covered by a white sheet, just glared. Not that anyone noticed — except for Jason, who was making himself look more perfect by the minute.

"Oh, hey there, Ben," he said on his way out of the kitchen, giving my big bro a friendly wave. "What's up?"

"I can walk on my hands!" Ben boasted, perhaps forgetting what had happened the last time he tried it. Jason just nodded politely. Guess he'd already learned the essential Singer household lesson: Sometimes when Ben talks, you should just pretend you're listening. And then run away. It was like Jason was already part of the family!

"What's this?" Mom asked, pointing to the thing under the sheet.

"I thought you'd never ask." As if he were a magician revealing his final trick, Ben whipped the sheet off, revealing ... uh, what was it? It was made out of wood, and it was kind of bulky, with lots of corners. Mom and Dad exchanged a glance, then quickly smiled at Ben, trying to look as proud as they did the day he brought home his very first misshapen Play-Doh sculpture from first-grade art class. He hadn't improved much since then.

"Ta-da!" Ben announced. "I built it with my own two hands. What do you think?"

"It's ... great," Dad said slowly. "Really, really ... great."

"Yes," Mom quickly agreed. "What a lovely doorstop."

Ben glowered. "It's a chair."

"Really?" But Mom covered up her surprise as fast as she could. "Uh, I mean, really, really nice."

"Guess you don't have to be a 'contractor' to build cool things, huh?" Ben patted the chair and waved Dad over. "Go ahead, Dad. Sit on it."

It was the last thing Dad wanted to do. But he did it, anyway. That's what makes him Dad.

"Wow, Ben," he said in a fake hearty voice, doing his best not to put all his weight on it. "This is fan —"

CRAAAAAACK!

The chair splintered into about a million pieces, sending Dad tumbling to the floor in a heap of broken wood. He lay there for a moment, clutching his back and moaning.

"Jeff, are you okay?" Mom asked, rushing over to kneel beside him.

"My back. Oooh, ow, my back . . ."

Enter Jason, contractor, surrogate son, and now superhero, come to save the day. "What happened?" he cried, barreling though the white plastic curtain. "Is everything okay?"

"I'm fine," Dad groaned, still sitting on the floor. "Just blew up a chair and twisted my back."

"May I?" And before anyone could answer, Jason

blew on his hands, clapped them together, and began rubbing them together. After a few seconds, he clapped one hand down on each of Dad's shoulders and began to knead.

"Please!" Ben muttered to himself. "Jason doesn't know anything about fixing backs —"

"Wow." Dad sighed with pleasure and leaned his head back, relaxing into the massage. "That's amazing. How'd you do that?"

"It's the Japanese art of shiatsu massage," Jason explained, continuing to knead the muscles. "I spent a summer in Kyoto, gardening with Zen monks."

"Aww," Mom and Dad gushed simultaneously.

And from the look on Ben's face, you could tell that I wasn't the only one with a green monster stirring inside.

"I bet he doesn't know anything about arm wrestling," Ben scoffed as he stalked out of the room.

Looks like someone needed to start the "Five Steps to Overcoming Jealousy." He could have my pamphlet — after all, I'd put the whole thing far, far behind me!

Or so I thought.

It happened in *Juice!* At first, everything was quiet, normal. Zach's friend from the basketball team was sitting at one table, trying to sell Cranberry one of his stuffed mascot bullfrogs.

"They're lightweight, durable, and washing-machine safe," he said.

"And kind of ugly," Cranberry pointed out.

"Haven't you heard? Ugly is the new pretty."

Cranberry flushed, and then fake-smiled as if she already knew that. "Oh, yeah, I know ... I totally read about that. I'm way ahead of you."

See? Cranberry was trying to pretend she knew everything, just like usual. And I was hanging with Geena and Zach, finally happy and relaxed for the first time all week, so things were getting back to normal there, too.

"Thanks so much for your help," I told them. "I feel totally in control now. I can't believe I was ever jealous in the first ..."

My voice trailed off. I stopped. I stared. I had spotted Randy up at the counter. Talking to the cute blond trainee. The one who'd given him a free smoothie. The one who'd wanted him. Who probably still did. I was sure of it.

"... place." I finished my sentence, but my mind was already someplace else. Someplace *angry*.

"You know the five steps she took forward?"

Zach asked Geena. "I think she's about to take fifteen steps back."

And he was right. I took fifteen fast, angry steps toward the counter, to get close enough to overhear their conversation and confirm my suspicions.

"Are you sure I can't pay you for the smoothie?" Randy asked, grinning gratefully.

"I'm positive." The *Juice!* trainee grinned back — and then, I'm almost positive, she *winked* at him! At *my* boyfriend! "Like I said before, your cute smile is —"

BAM!

The trainee didn't get to finish her sentence, because I had pelted her in the face with a stuffed frog. "He's taken, blondie!" I shouted, scooping up more frogs. Ammunition, you know. The big green monster had come out to play. And she was *mad*.

"Uh, Addie?" Zach's friend said timidly. "We pretty much have a 'you chuck it at a person's head, you buy it' policy. . . ."

Randy wasn't so timid. More like stunned. "Addie, what're you doing?"

What was I doing? I was walking closer and closer to the counter, throwing bullfrog after bullfrog at the trainee. She tried to block them, but I was too fast for

95

her. She disappeared behind the counter, and I thought I'd won — but then she popped up again with . . . uh-oh.

Two cans of whipped cream, aimed right at me! I ducked, but she sprayed and sprayed, covering me with a sticky white cloud.

"Ha-ha! Take that!" she cried.

I stumbled backward, bumping against a table where a couple of kids were sharing a big bowl of sorbet. Perfect. I stole one of their spoons, got a big scoop of sorbet, and flicked it at the trainee.

Bull's-eye!

"Yeah, how do you like me now?" I jeered, wiping whipped cream off of my face so I could take better aim. My vision cleared just in time to get a better view of the stream of wheatgrass juice flying toward me from the hose the trainee had pointed in my direction.

"Eat wheatgrass, psycho girl!" she shouted, drenching me in the nasty-smelling liquid.

I was soaked, sticky, and not nearly ready to quit. I grabbed some muffins off the first table I saw and hurled them toward the trainee. Direct hit, yes!

She sprayed more juice at me, and I flung more food at her, and both of us looked like we'd been stuck in the blender and mixed in with a smoothie when —

"STOP!" Randy stepped in between us, raising his

arms and staring at me in horror. We both froze. There was a look on Randy's face I'd never seen before. That cute smile was nowhere to be seen. Instead he looked serious. He looked sorry. "That's it," he said, more quietly. "I really like you, Addie, but I can't take this anymore. I want to break up."

"Randy, wait!" I cried. But he walked out of the café, and out of my life. Before I could say anything else, or follow him . . .

WHAP! An orange slammed into my head and knocked me to the ground.

"Yes!" the trainee cheered, pumping her sorbet-covered fist in the air. "Two points!"

That's when the manager finally showed up and discovered what we had done to the place. He glared at the trainee, speechless for a moment. But only a moment. "You are *so* on probation."

As for me? I just lay there on the floor, covered in wheatgrass juice and whipped cream, stunned. All at once, I realized what I had done. I had gone completely overboard — crazy. I had driven Randy away. And for what? None of those girls were a threat to our relationship.

Turns out, the only threat was me.

Ben had decided it was time to take matters into his own hands. Literally. He found Jason measuring one of the new walls in the addition. He didn't say anything at first, just stood there and waited for Jason to notice him.

"Hey, Ben," Jason said when he finally turned around. "What's up?"

But Ben still didn't say anything. He just stood there and stared. Then, finally, he pulled a baseball cap out of his back pocket and slid it onto his head. Backward.

I think he was trying to intimidate Jason — but probably, he was just creeping him out.

Ben walked slowly toward the kitchen, gesturing for Jason to follow. When they passed under the white plastic curtain, Ben sat down at the kitchen table and planted his elbow on it. He raised his fist in the classic arm-wrestling challenge position.

His eyes narrowed to slits. "Let's see whatcha got, wunderkind."

Taking his cue from Ben, Jason didn't say anything, either. He just sat down at the table across from Ben and got into position. They grasped hands, silently counted to three, and then —

Jason slammed Ben's hand down to the table in less than five seconds.

Ben raised his fist, ready to go again.

This time, he lost in less than three seconds.

Again and again, and each time Ben's knuckles thudded painfully into the table as Jason bested him.

Was there nothing he couldn't do?

When I got home that night, my clothes smelled like a lawn mower, and so did I. That was thanks to the wheatgrass.

My heart felt like a big, cold stone. That was thanks to Randy Klein.

The green-eyed monster got ahold of me, I sang mournfully to myself as I showered three times in a row trying to scrub off all the whipped cream.

Oh, jealousy.
He turned me into something I swore I'd never be.
Oh, jealousy.
It wasn't you, now I see. It was insecurity.
The green-eyed monster made a fool of me.
Oh, jealousy.

Jason was poring over some blueprints at the kitchen table while Mom prepared him a special treat.

"So we should have the floor installed in the next few days," he said.

"Jason, that's great news!" she exclaimed, setting a tray of hot cocoa and cookies down next to him. Ben walked into the kitchen, caught sight of Jason, and then immediately turned around to leave again.

"Ben, what happened to your wrist?" Mom asked, noticing that his right wrist was bound up with an Ace bandage.

"Nothing!" Ben protested. Like, way to make it obvious that you have something to hide. "The sun was in my eyes! I fell off my bike! I'll be in my room!" He glared at Jason. "Which *you* don't know anything about."

Mom shrugged and urged Jason to take a cookie. He did. No one can resist my Mom's chocolate chip cookies.

"Thanks for all your hospitality, Mrs. Singer," he said, taking a big bite.

Mom blushed. "Oh, it's the least I can do."

"You know, you remind me of someone very special to me."

"Really? Who?"

"My grandma."

Uh-oh. Looked like Jason wasn't so perfect after all. Or at least, not so smart. My mother's smile froze on her face. "Excuse me?"

"She's so warm and giving, just like you," Jason went on, oblivious to the fact that my mother was squeezing her cookie so hard it had crumbled into cookie dust. "In fact, her birthday is next week, and I'm still not sure what to get her. What do women of your generation like?"

"*My* generation?"

I won't tell you what happened next. Let's just say it wasn't pretty — and by dinnertime, Mr. Perfect Contractor had disappeared.

"Is Jason here?" Dad asked as soon as he came home. "I brought home one of those Ultimate Frisbees I was telling him about."

Mom didn't even look up from stirring her pot of

stew. She just shook her head and said, as casually as possible, "No, I fired him."

"What?" Dad gestured to the plastic curtain hanging from the ceiling. "We don't have a wall! We're in the middle of construction and you fired our contractor, our great, great contractor? Why?" His voice was rising, and you could tell all the blood was rushing to his head. He looked about ready to either explode or pass out. "Why did you do that?"

"He told me I reminded him of his grandmother," Mom said simply.

'Nuff said.

"Okay, well, I'll start looking for someone new in the morning," Dad said calmly. He knew what was good for him.

"Mom, you look like you could be my older sister," Ben said smarmily. He knew what was good for *him*, too.

Mom smiled lovingly at him. "My sweet, sweet boy," she gushed.

Ben nodded to himself. All was right with the world. "Jason *sure* doesn't know anything about women," he murmured.

And thank goodness for that.

*   *   *

School was lonelier the next day. On the surface, everything was the same, I guess. But *nothing* was the same. Because suddenly, I was alone. The worst part was when I spotted Randy down the hall, stuffing some books into his locker. I really wanted to talk to him. More than anything, I just wanted to turn back the clock and start the whole week over. But I didn't know how to do that. So I stayed where I was, all alone.

Well, not *all* alone. Because as I was standing there, Jake Behari came up behind me and tapped me on the shoulder. "Hey, Addie."

A couple months ago, I would have been ecstatic to see him. I would have been dancing down the hallway, overcome with joy that *he* had come up to *me*. I would have struggled for something to say because I was too busy dreaming of how handsome we would look out on our first date. Or maybe at our wedding.

But like I said, everything felt different now. And when I saw Jake, I couldn't even bring myself to smile. "Hey, Jake," I said flatly.

"Haven't seen you in a while. How's it going?"

"Not too good, actually," I admitted. For some reason, now that I don't *like* Jake anymore — at least not *that* way — it's a lot easier to talk to him. We're actually friends now, and I can say anything to him. Even this: "Randy broke up with me and probably never wants to see me again."

Jake had a weird expression on his face. I couldn't read it. But all he said was, "Well, do *you* want to see *him*?"

I sighed. "Yeah, I do." Not that it mattered. Not anymore.

"Then you should talk to him," Jake urged me. "Before it's too late."

Could he be right? I looked at Randy again — he was still at his locker. He hadn't seen me yet. What would he do if I actually tried to talk to him? Yell at me? Run away? I guess it didn't matter. Whatever he did, it wouldn't be worse than the way I was feeling, just watching him from far away. Jake gave me an encouraging smile and, for the first time in days, I smiled back. And then I took a deep breath and walked slowly down the hall, stopping in front of Randy's locker.

"Hey."

He looked at me and, for a second, it seemed like he wanted to smile, but he didn't. "Hi."

And then there was just this really awkward pause. I knew he was waiting for me to say something, and I was really wishing that *he* would say something. But I was the one who'd messed up — so I guess it was only fair that I was the one who went first.

"Look, I know you probably never want to talk to me again after the way I've acted, but I just wanted to say I'm sorry," I spit out all in one breath. At least I'd said it. Now it was just a question of whether he'd accept my apology. Whether we could fix things.

"You kind of just went crazy."

"I know. I just . . ." I gave him a weak smile. "I guess I just never noticed the way girls flirted with you all the time. I mean, you could date anyone you wanted. . . ."

"I *was* dating anyone I wanted. You."

What? I couldn't believe it — and I didn't know what to say. So it's a good thing Randy kept talking.

"You're the only Addie Singer I know. I really like you."

"I like you, too," I said, suddenly feeling a little shy.

Randy looked down for a second and shifted his weight back and forth, like he was nervous. Join the club. "So, um, do you want to eat lunch together?" he finally asked.

Did I? Yes! YES! Definitely! Without a doubt!

"Um, yeah," I said out loud, quietly and calmly,

like he hadn't just made my heart practically leap out of my body. "So, does this mean you want to, like, get back together?"

There was another pause, and this one felt like it lasted a thousand years. And then, finally, Randy smiled. And I could breathe again.

"Yeah. As long as you promise to go back to being the old, fun Addie." He held out his hand, and I took it.

"I promise." We shook on it — and he didn't let go.

As we stood there together, hand in hand, Patti, Maris, and Cranberry walked by, giggling and goggling. "Hi, Randy!" the three of them said together, each giving him a cutesy little wave.

Randy looked at me, waiting to see how I would react.

"How do they talk in unison like that?" I joked, giving Randy a mischievous grin. "Pretty impressive."

"They must practice," he suggested — and I could tell he was relieved.

I'd passed my first test. And you know what? It was easy. I didn't have to fake it or anything — because suddenly, I really didn't care anymore. Let the girls think he was cute. Let them giggle and flirt. It didn't matter — Randy said he wanted to be with *me*. And I trusted him — and that was all that counted.

We walked down the hall, holding hands, just like old times. As we passed by Jake, I winked at him, and mouthed, "Thank you." Randy and I were happy again, and I owed it all to him. Jake waved back, but he didn't smile — and he had that same expression on his face from before, the one I couldn't figure out. It looked sort of familiar, like I'd seen it somewhere else . . . like I'd seen it in the mirror. If I didn't know any better, I realized, I would think that the green-eyed monster was stirring somewhere deep inside Jake Behari — that as he watched us walk down the hall together, he was jealous. Of me!

That's what I'd think, at least, if I didn't know any better. But I do — know better, that is. Jake couldn't possibly be jealous of Randy and me. . . .

Could he?

PLAY THE GAME!

Help Addie navigate the hectic halls of Rocky Road Middle School and avoid becoming popularity roadkill in an all-new adventure for the Game Boy Advance.

COMING FALL 2006

GAME BOY ADVANCE

www.nick.com

THQ

www.thq.com